TRANSFORMERS

DARK OF THE MOON

RISING STORM

VOLUME 4

STORY BY **JOHN BARBER**

ART BY **CARLOS MAGNO**

COLORS BY **ABURTOV** AND **GRAPHIKSLAVA**

LETTERS BY **CHRIS MOWRY** AND **SHAWN LEE**

SERIES ASSISTANT EDITOR **CARLOS GUZMAN**

SERIES EDITOR **ANDY SCHMIDT**

COLLECTION EDITOR **JUSTIN EISINGER**

COLLECTION DESIGNER **SHAWN LEE**

Licensed By:

visit us at www.abdopublishing.com

Reinforced library bound edition published in 2012 by Spotlight,
a division of the ABDO Group, PO Box 398166, Minneapolis, MN 55439.
Spotlight produces high-quality reinforced library bound editions for schools and
libraries. Published by agreement with IDW Publishing. www.idwpublishing.com

Printed in the United States of America, North Mankato, Minnesota.
102011
012012
♲ This book contains at least 10% recycled materials.

Library of Congress Cataloging-in-Publication Data

Barber, John, 1976-
 Dark of the moon : rising storm / story by John Barber ; art by Carlos Magno ;
letters by Chris Mowry.
    p. cm. -- (Transformers, dark of the moon movie prequel)
 ISBN 978-1-59961-975-0 (volume 1) -- ISBN 978-1-59961-976-7 (volume 2) --
ISBN 978-1-59961-977-4 (volume 3) -- ISBN 978-1-59961-978-1 (volume 4)
 1. Graphic novels. I. Magno, Carlos, 1976- II. Transformers, dark of the moon
(Motion picture) III. Title. IV. Title: Rising storm.
 PZ7.7.B35Tr 2012
 741.5'973--dc23

                            2011029798

All Spotlight books are reinforced library binding
and manufactured in the United States of America.

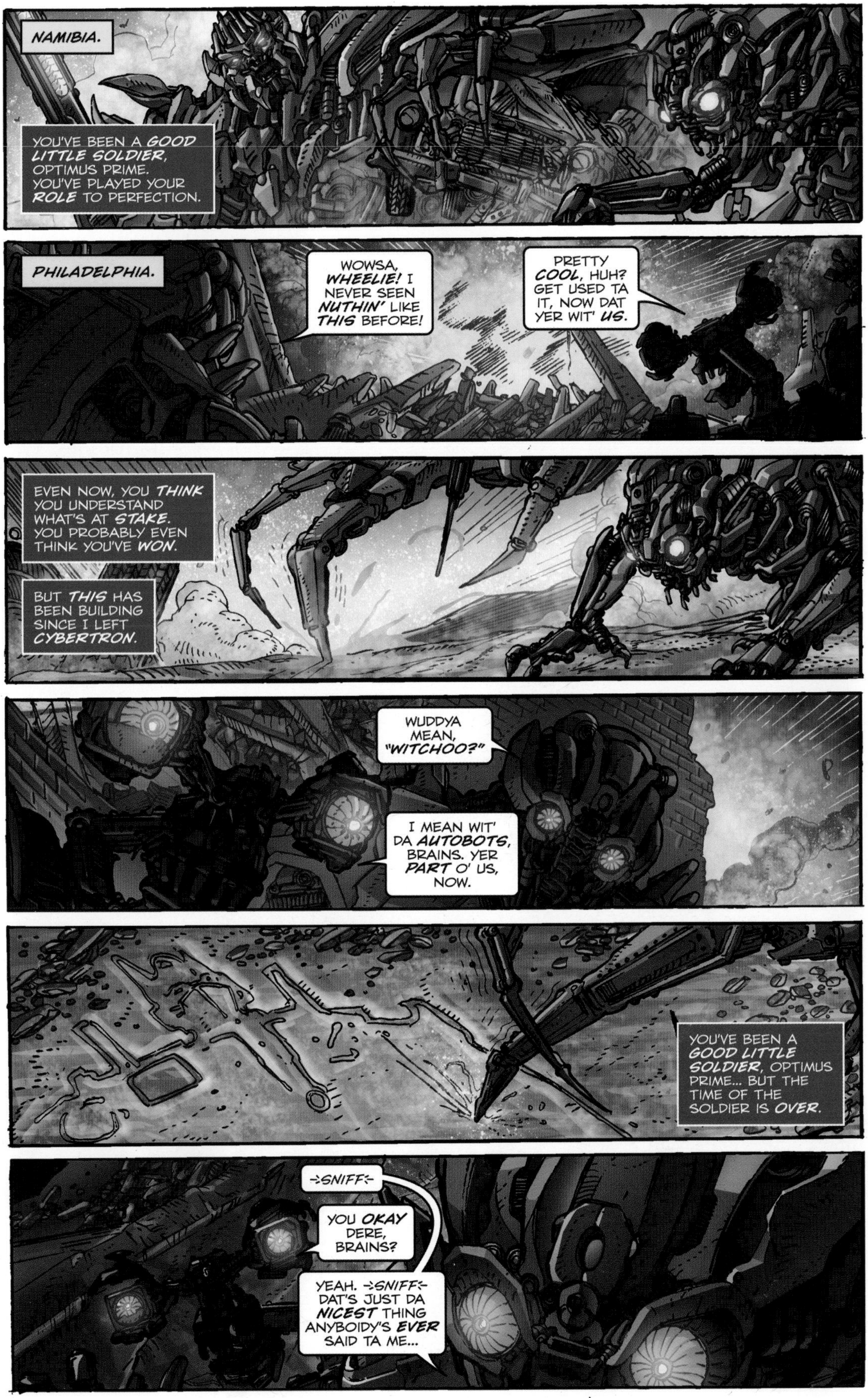

NAMIBIA.
YOU'VE BEEN A GOOD LITTLE SOLDIER, OPTIMUS PRIME. YOU'VE PLAYED YOUR ROLE TO PERFECTION.
PHILADELPHIA.
WOWSA, WHEELIE! I NEVER SEEN NUTHIN' LIKE THIS BEFORE!
PRETTY COOL, HUH? GET USED TA IT, NOW DAT YER WIT' US.
EVEN NOW, YOU THINK YOU UNDERSTAND WHAT'S AT STAKE. YOU PROBABLY EVEN THINK YOU'VE WON.
BUT THIS HAS BEEN BUILDING SINCE I LEFT CYBERTRON.
WUDDYA MEAN, "WITCHOO?"
I MEAN WIT' DA AUTOBOTS, BRAINS. YER PART O' US, NOW.
YOU'VE BEEN A GOOD LITTLE SOLDIER, OPTIMUS PRIME... BUT THE TIME OF THE SOLDIER IS OVER.
-SNIFF-
YOU OKAY DERE, BRAINS?
YEAH. -SNIFF- DAT'S JUST DA NICEST THING ANYBOIDY'S EVER SAID TA ME...

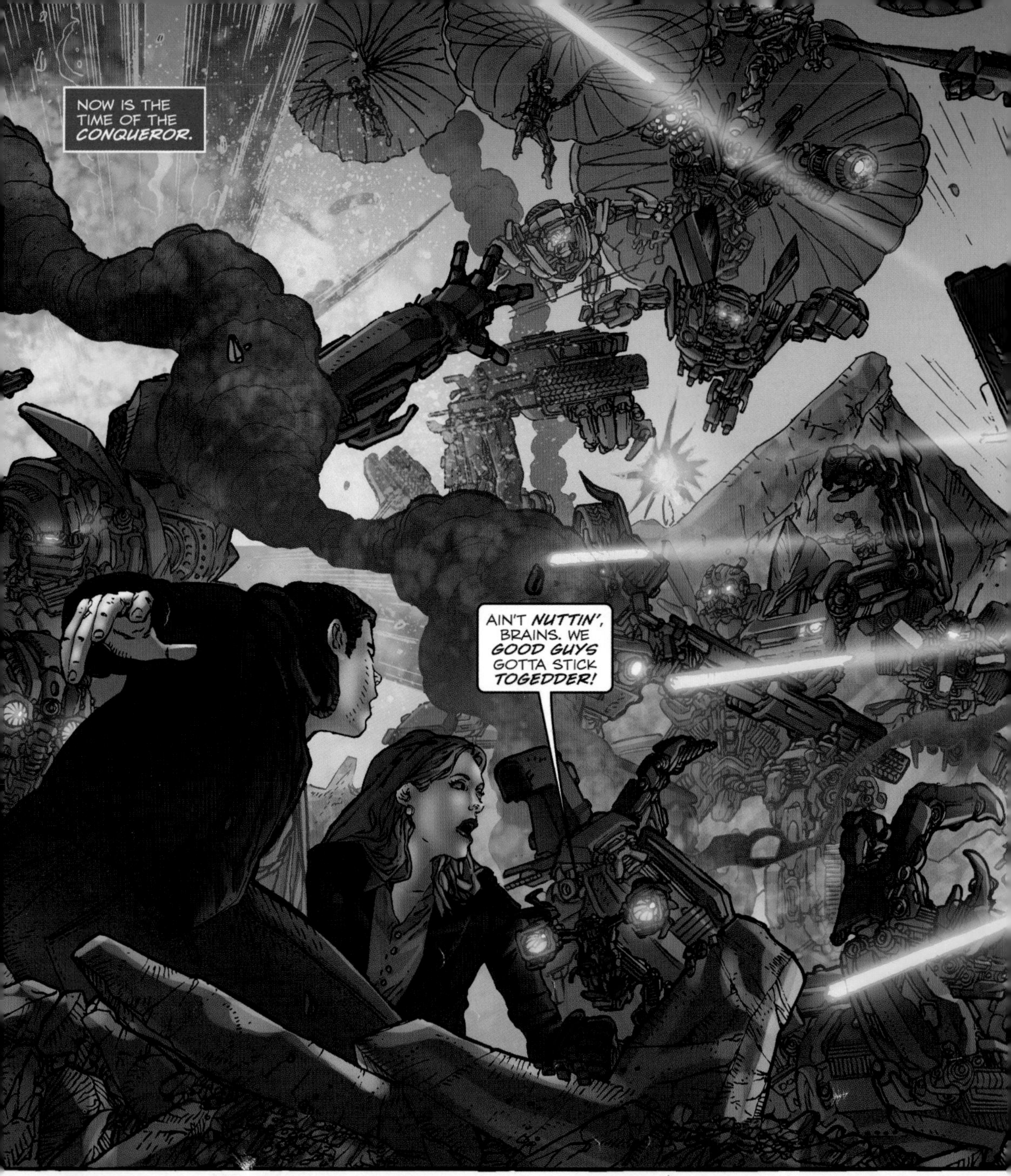
NOW IS THE TIME OF THE CONQUEROR.
AIN'T NUTTIN', BRAINS. WE GOOD GUYS GOTTA STICK TOGEDDER!
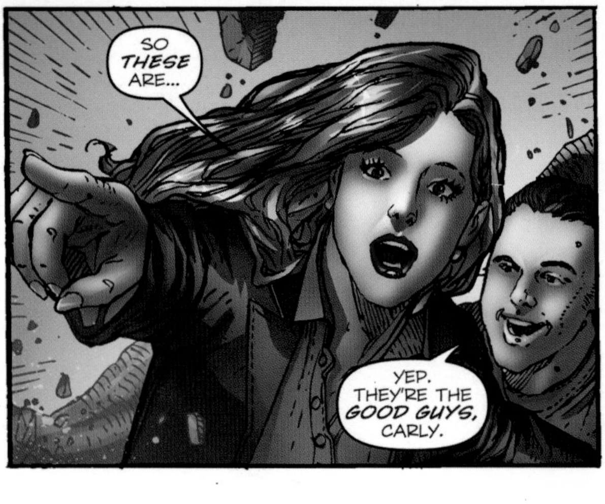
SO THESE ARE...
YEP. THEY'RE THE GOOD GUYS, CARLY.
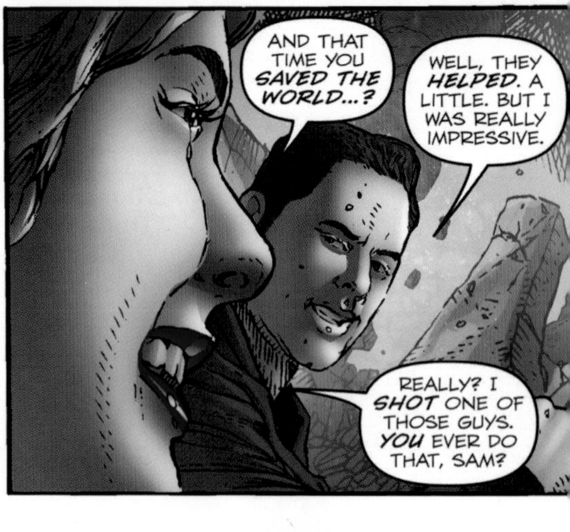
AND THAT TIME YOU SAVED THE WORLD...?
WELL, THEY HELPED. A LITTLE. BUT I WAS REALLY IMPRESSIVE.
REALLY? I SHOT ONE OF THOSE GUYS. YOU EVER DO THAT, SAM?

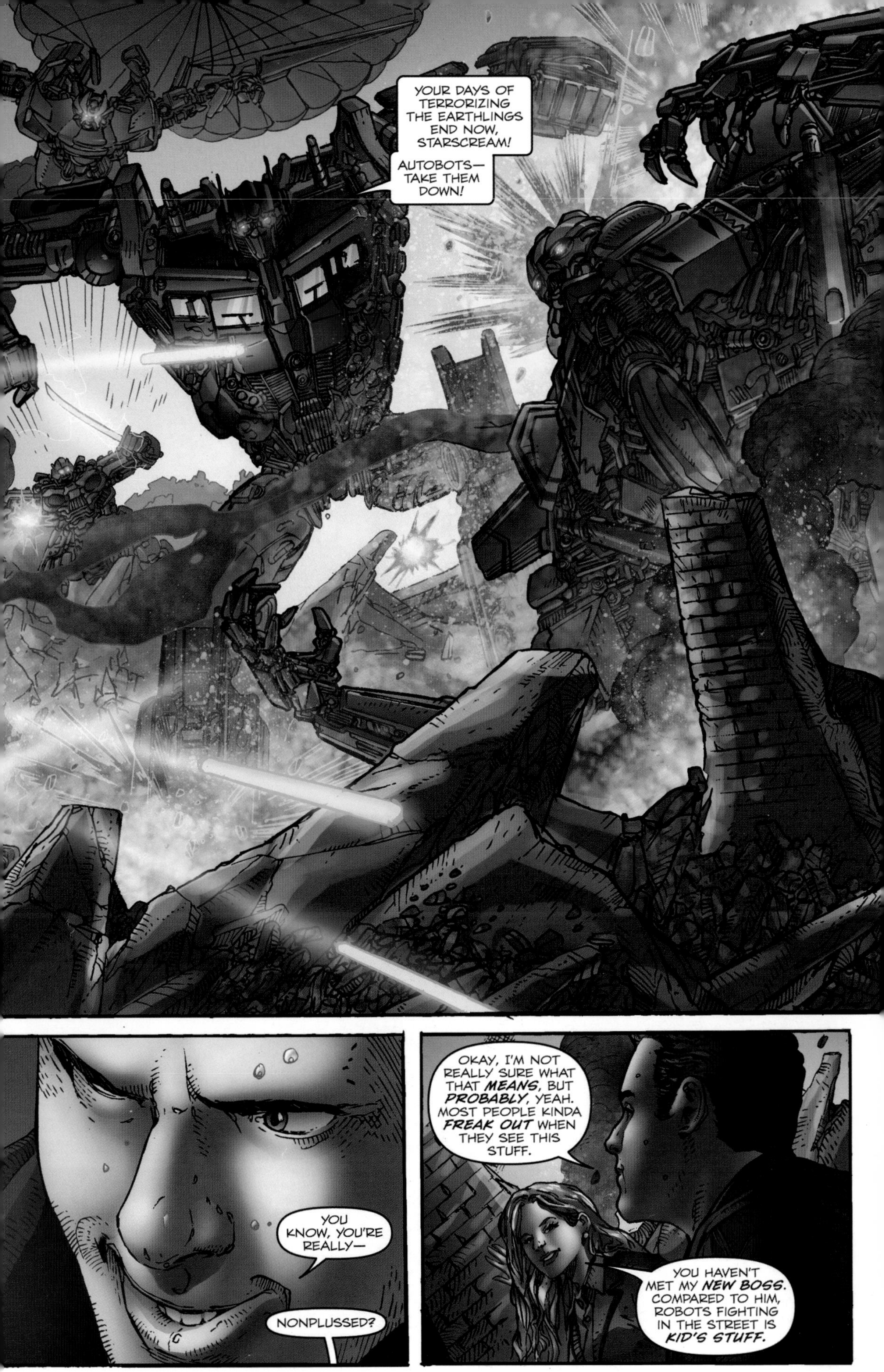
YOUR DAYS OF TERRORIZING THE EARTHLINGS END NOW, STARSCREAM!
AUTOBOTS— TAKE THEM DOWN!
YOU KNOW, YOU'RE REALLY—
NONPLUSSED?
OKAY, I'M NOT REALLY SURE WHAT THAT **MEANS**, BUT **PROBABLY**, YEAH. MOST PEOPLE KINDA **FREAK OUT** WHEN THEY SEE THIS STUFF.
YOU HAVEN'T MET MY **NEW BOSS**. COMPARED TO HIM, ROBOTS FIGHTING IN THE STREET IS **KID'S STUFF.**

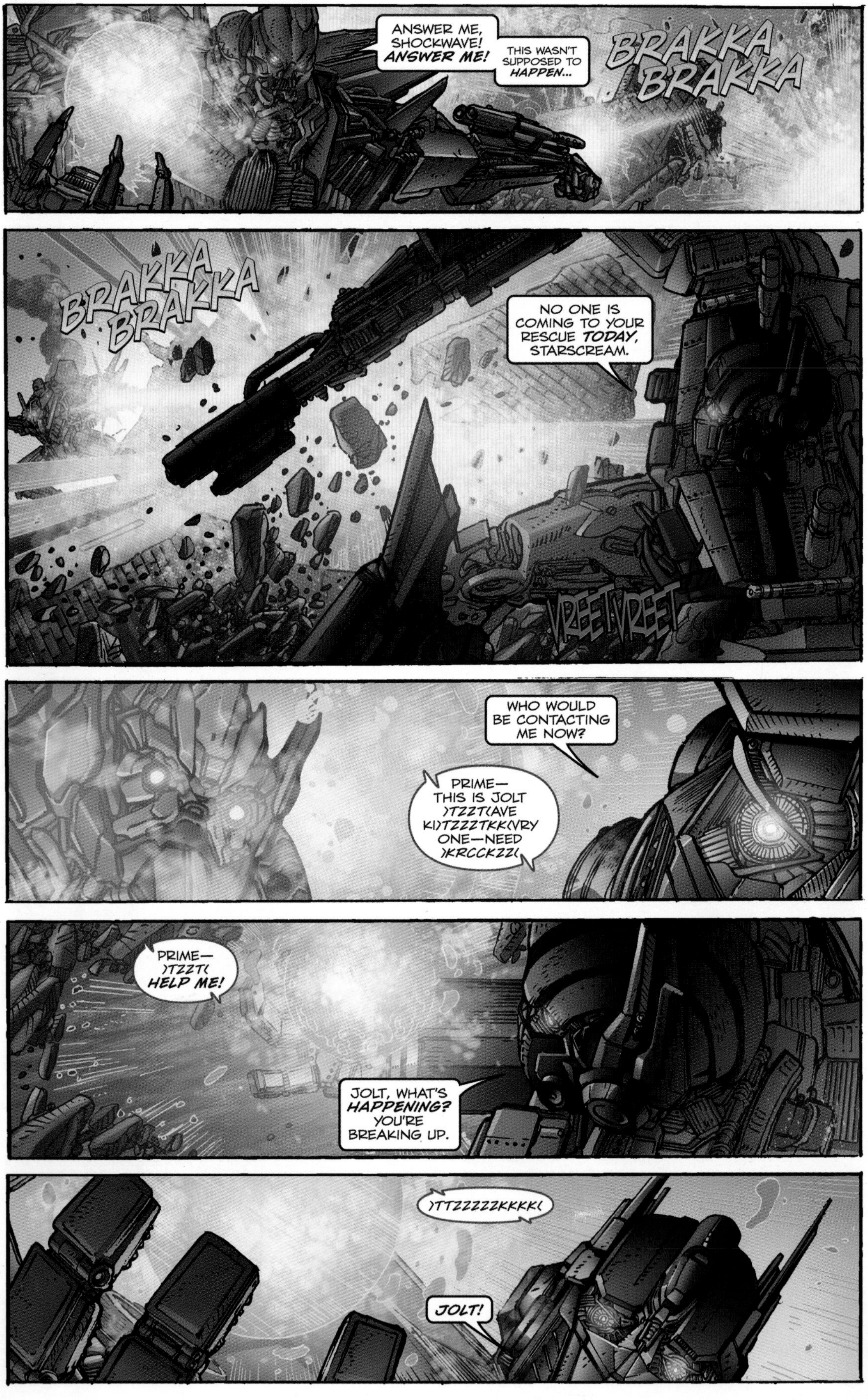
ANSWER ME, SHOCKWAVE! ANSWER ME!
THIS WASN'T SUPPOSED TO HAPPEN...
BRAKKA BRAKKA
BRAKKA BRAKKA
NO ONE IS COMING TO YOUR RESCUE TODAY, STARSCREAM.
VREETVREET
WHO WOULD BE CONTACTING ME NOW?
PRIME— THIS IS JOLT)TZZT(AVE KI)TZZZTKK(VRY ONE—NEED)KRCCKZZ(
PRIME—)TZZT(HELP ME!
JOLT, WHAT'S HAPPENING? YOU'RE BREAKING UP.
)TTZZZZZKKKK(
JOLT!

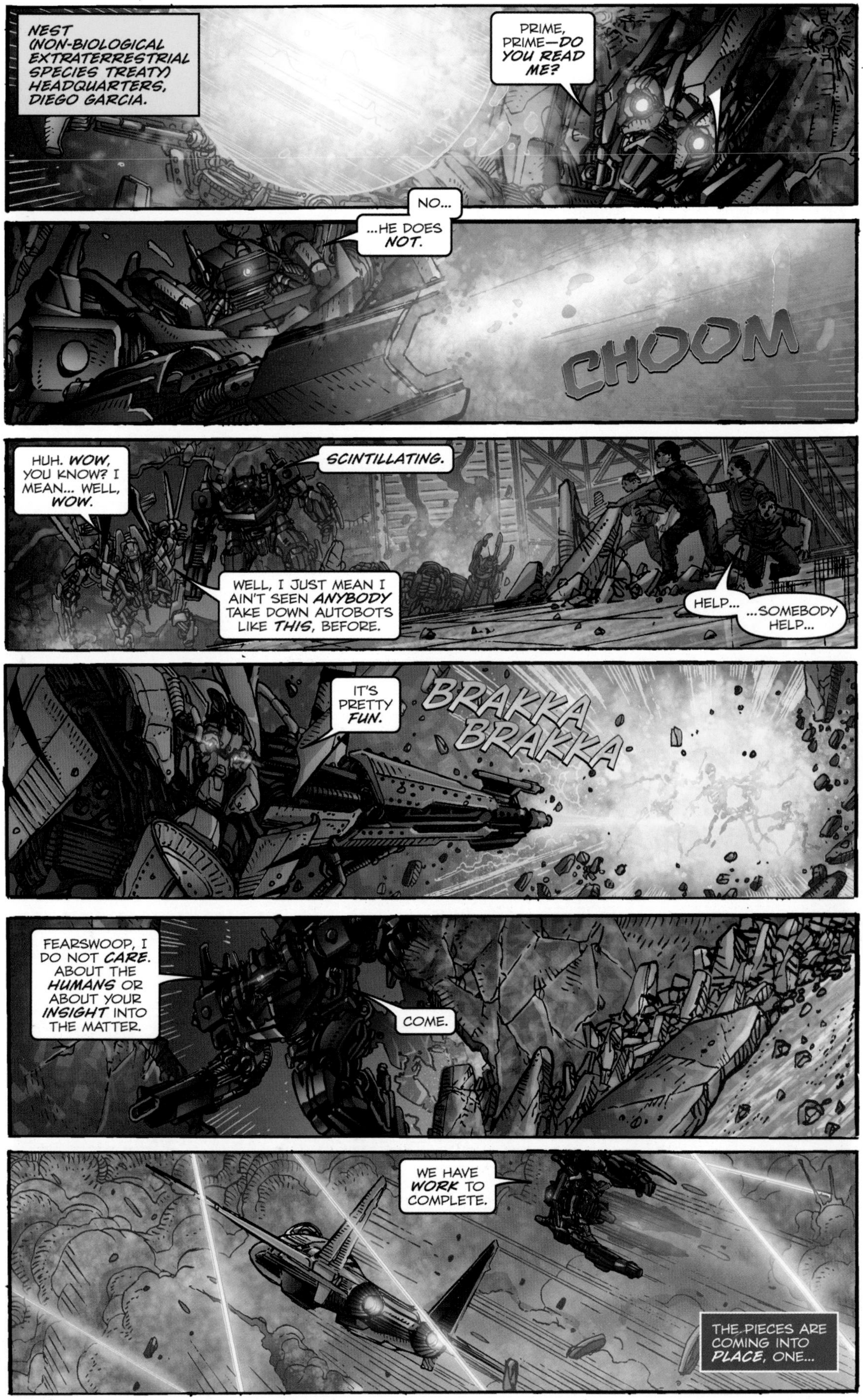
NEST (NON-BIOLOGICAL EXTRATERRESTRIAL SPECIES TREATY) HEADQUARTERS, DIEGO GARCIA.
PRIME, PRIME—DO YOU READ ME?
NO...
...HE DOES NOT.
CHOOM
HUH. WOW, YOU KNOW? I MEAN... WELL, WOW.
SCINTILLATING.
WELL, I JUST MEAN I AIN'T SEEN ANYBODY TAKE DOWN AUTOBOTS LIKE THIS, BEFORE.
HELP...
...SOMEBODY HELP...
IT'S PRETTY FUN.
BRAKKA BRAKKA
FEARSWOOP, I DO NOT CARE. ABOUT THE HUMANS OR ABOUT YOUR INSIGHT INTO THE MATTER.
COME.
WE HAVE WORK TO COMPLETE.
THE PIECES ARE COMING INTO PLACE, ONE...

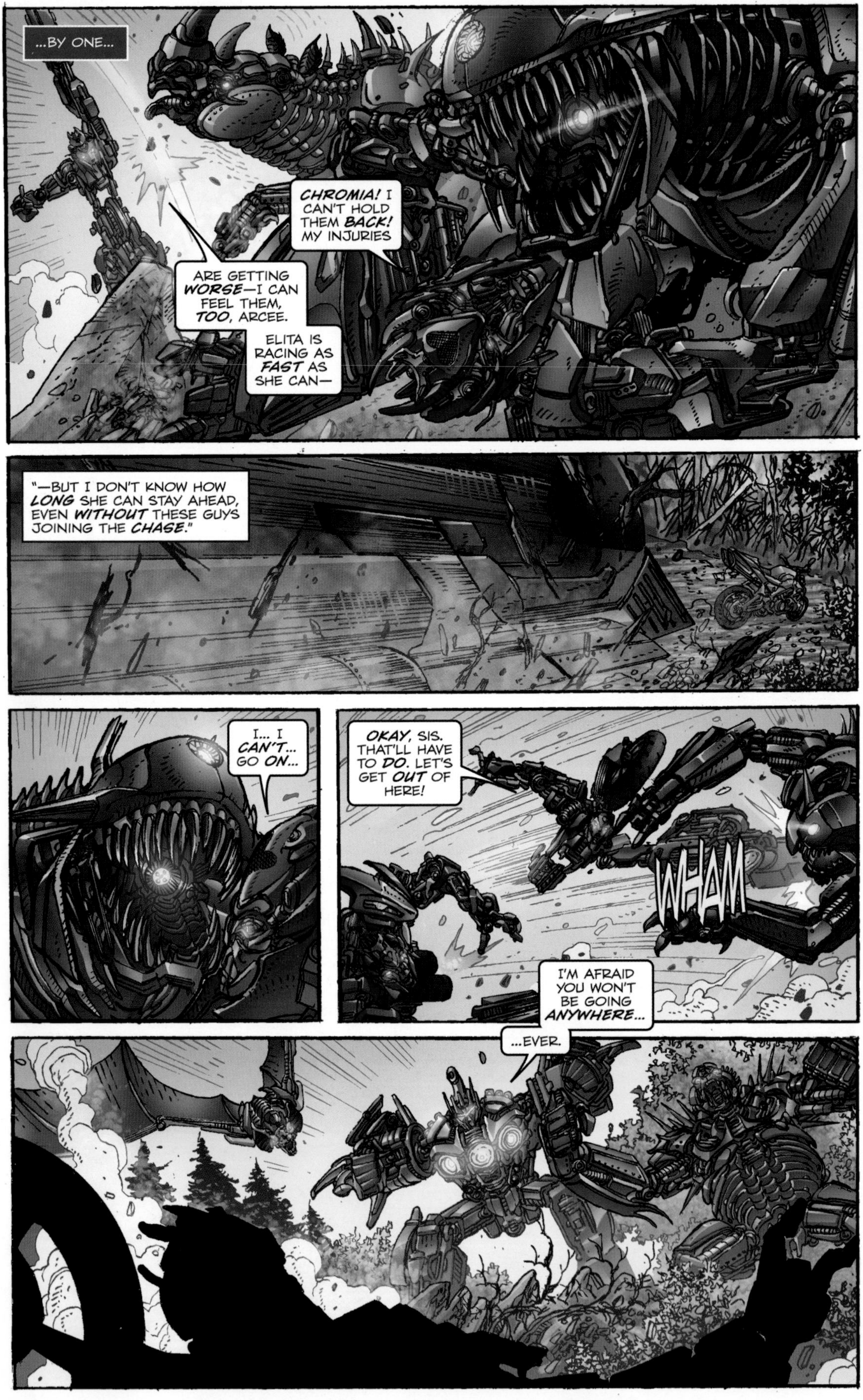
...BY ONE...
CHROMIA! I CAN'T HOLD THEM BACK! MY INJURIES
ARE GETTING WORSE—I CAN FEEL THEM, TOO, ARCEE.
ELITA IS RACING AS FAST AS SHE CAN—
"—BUT I DON'T KNOW HOW LONG SHE CAN STAY AHEAD, EVEN WITHOUT THESE GUYS JOINING THE CHASE."
I... I CAN'T... GO ON...
OKAY, SIS. THAT'LL HAVE TO DO. LET'S GET OUT OF HERE!
WHAM
I'M AFRAID YOU WON'T BE GOING ANYWHERE...
...EVER.

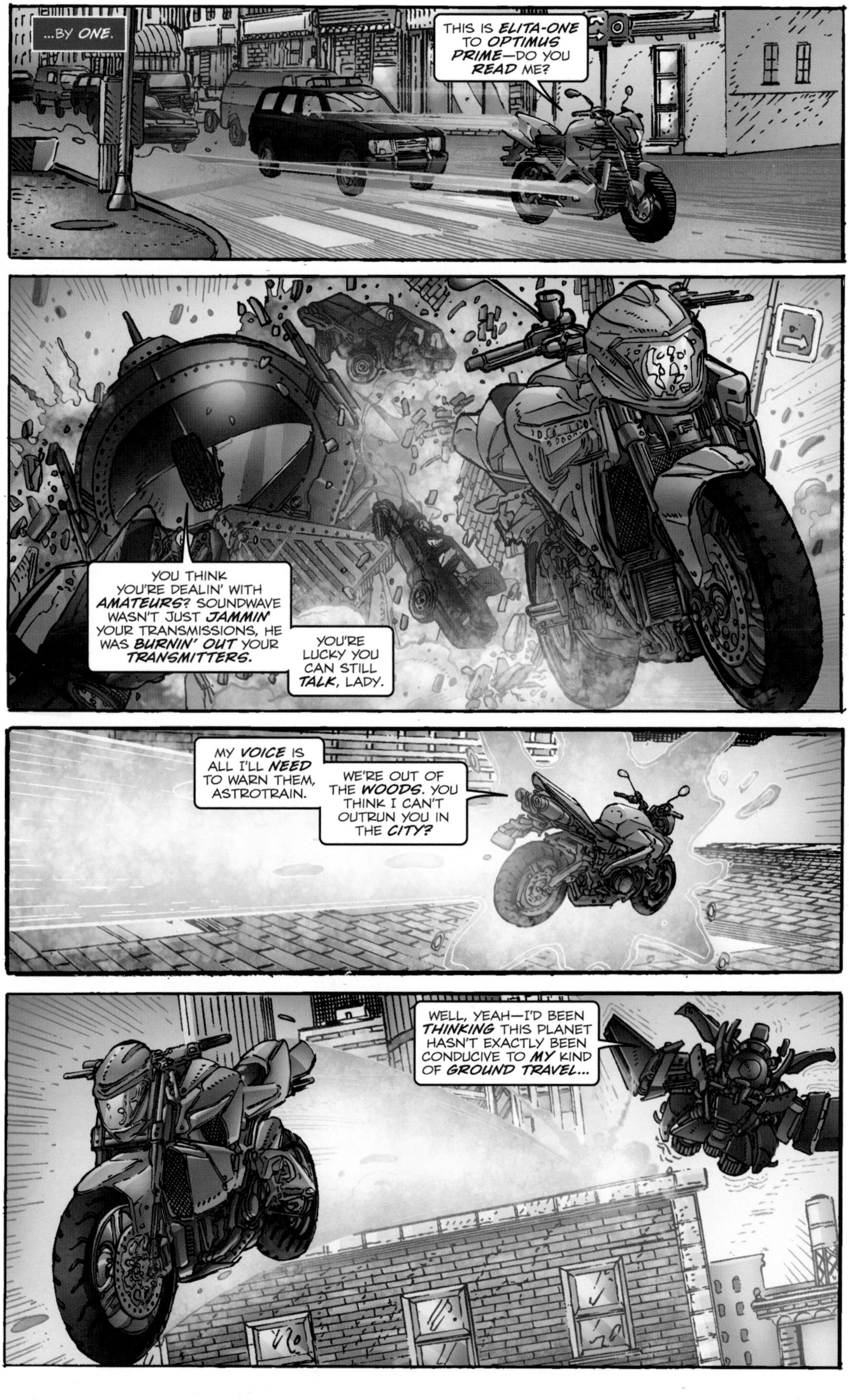
...BY ONE.
THIS IS ELITA-ONE TO OPTIMUS PRIME—DO YOU READ ME?
YOU THINK YOU'RE DEALIN' WITH AMATEURS? SOUNDWAVE WASN'T JUST JAMMIN' YOUR TRANSMISSIONS, HE WAS BURNIN' OUT YOUR TRANSMITTERS.
YOU'RE LUCKY YOU CAN STILL TALK, LADY.
MY VOICE IS ALL I'LL NEED TO WARN THEM, ASTROTRAIN.
WE'RE OUT OF THE WOODS. YOU THINK I CAN'T OUTRUN YOU IN THE CITY?
WELL, YEAH—I'D BEEN THINKING THIS PLANET HASN'T EXACTLY BEEN CONDUCIVE TO MY KIND OF GROUND TRAVEL...

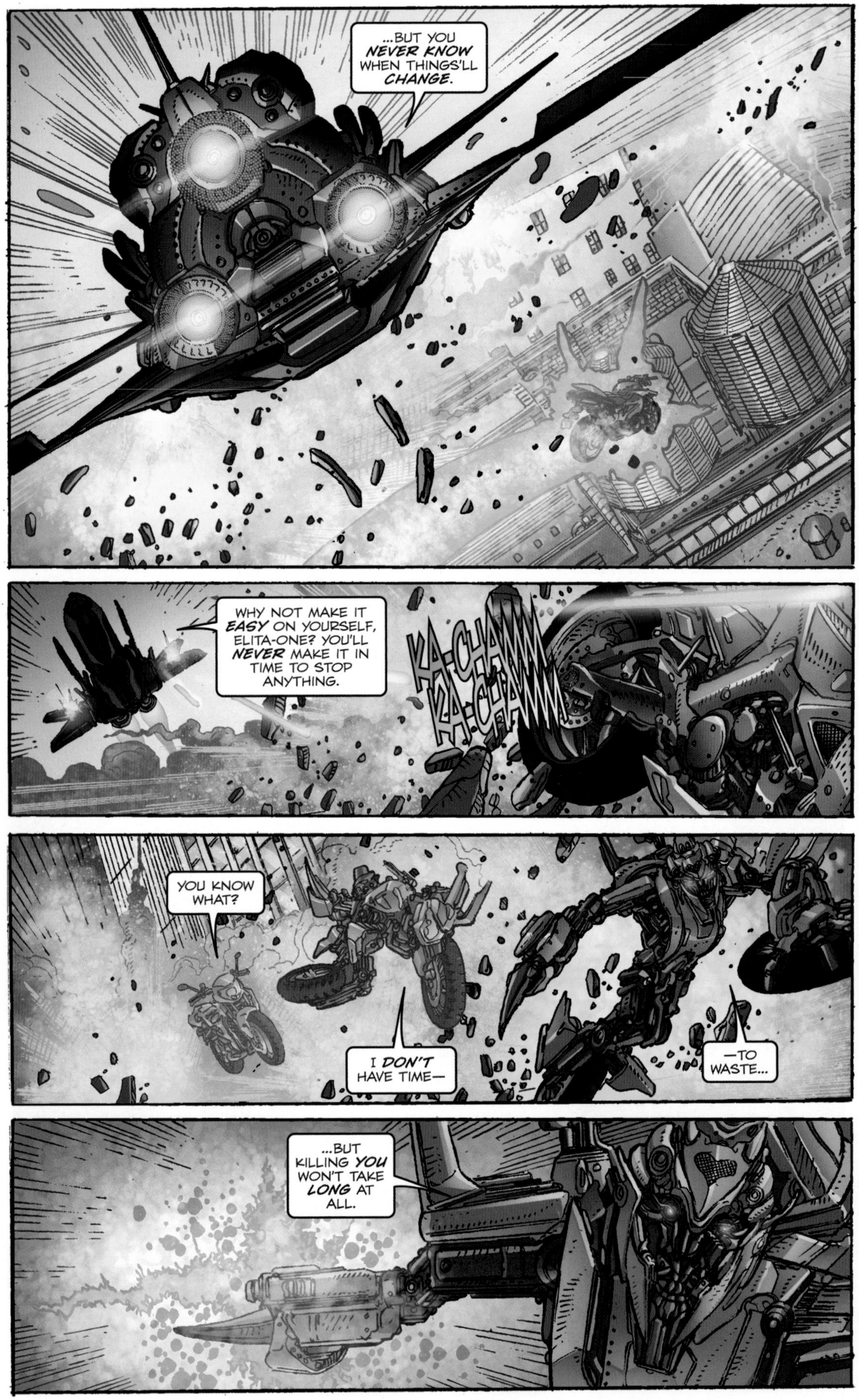
...BUT YOU NEVER KNOW WHEN THINGS'LL CHANGE.
WHY NOT MAKE IT EASY ON YOURSELF, ELITA-ONE? YOU'LL NEVER MAKE IT IN TIME TO STOP ANYTHING.
KA-CHAM
KA-CHAM
YOU KNOW WHAT?
I DON'T HAVE TIME—
—TO WASTE...
...BUT KILLING YOU WON'T TAKE LONG AT ALL.

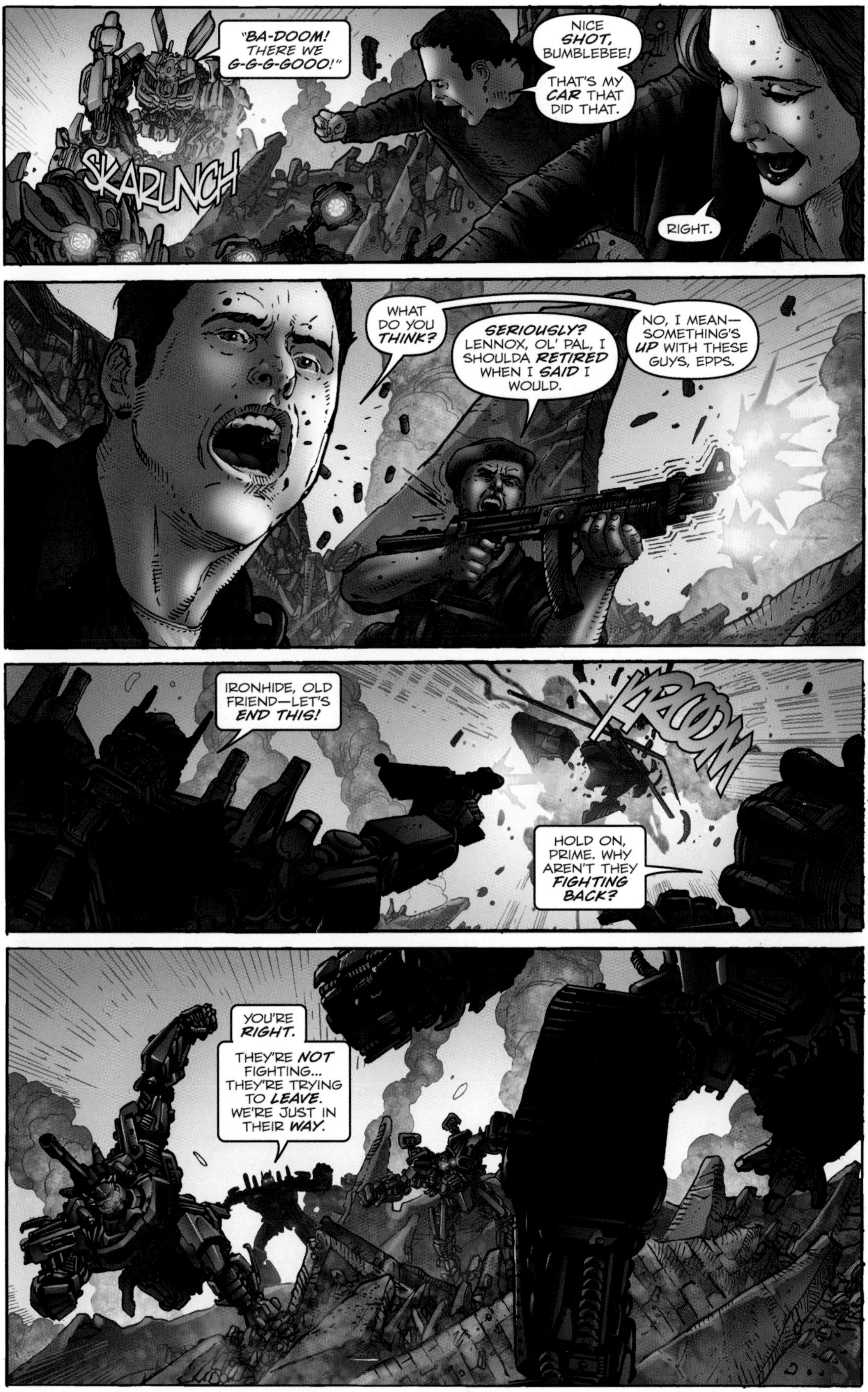
"BA-DOOM! THERE WE G-G-G-GOOO!"
SKARUNCH
NICE SHOT, BUMBLEBEE!
THAT'S MY CAR THAT DID THAT.
RIGHT.
WHAT DO YOU THINK?
SERIOUSLY? LENNOX, OL' PAL, I SHOULDA RETIRED WHEN I SAID I WOULD.
NO, I MEAN—SOMETHING'S UP WITH THESE GUYS, EPPS.
IRONHIDE, OLD FRIEND—LET'S END THIS!
VROOM
HOLD ON, PRIME. WHY AREN'T THEY FIGHTING BACK?
YOU'RE RIGHT.
THEY'RE NOT FIGHTING... THEY'RE TRYING TO LEAVE. WE'RE JUST IN THEIR WAY.

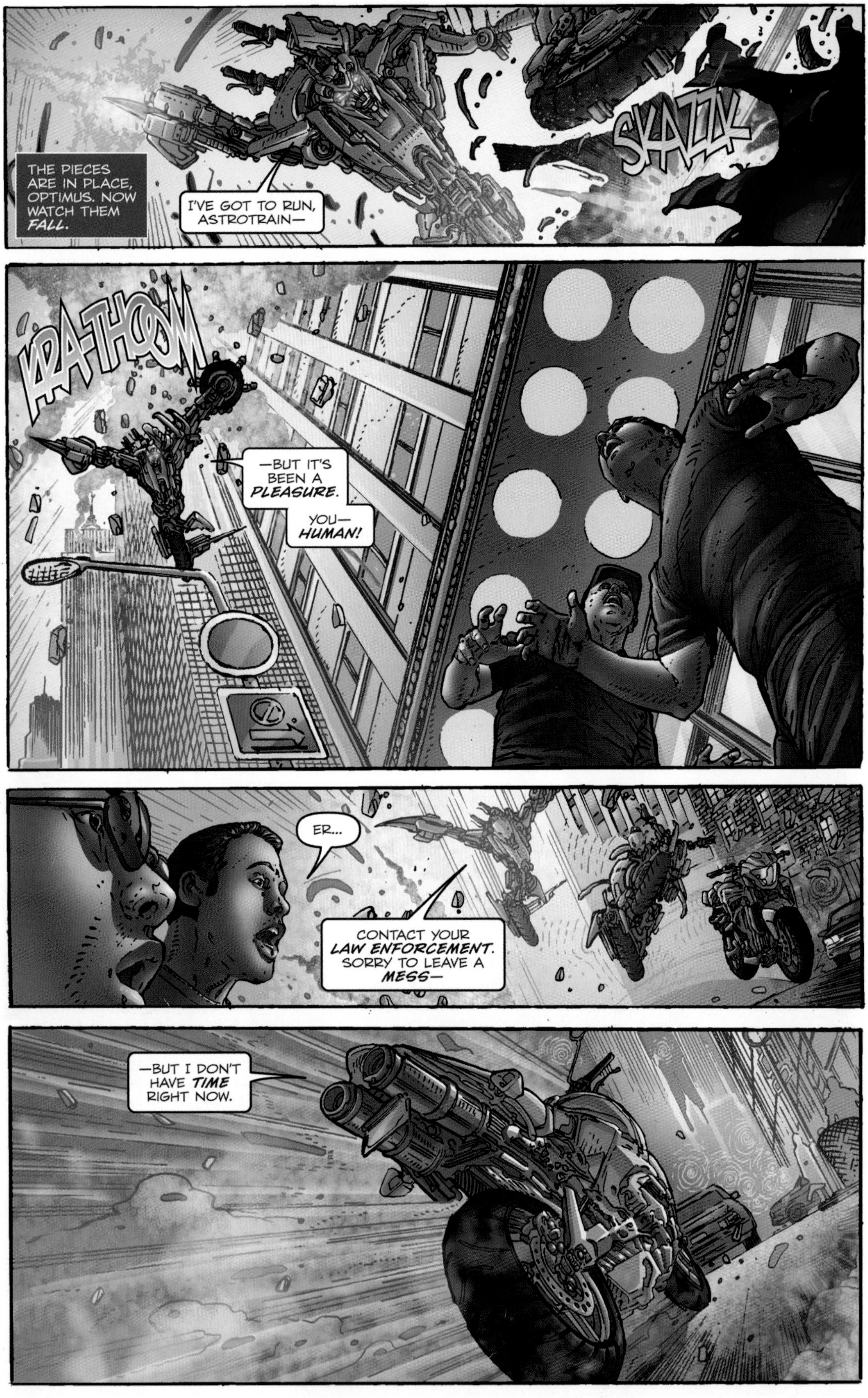
THE PIECES ARE IN PLACE, OPTIMUS. NOW WATCH THEM FALL.
I'VE GOT TO RUN, ASTROTRAIN—
SKAZZK
KRA-THOOM
—BUT IT'S BEEN A PLEASURE.
YOU— HUMAN!
ER...
CONTACT YOUR LAW ENFORCEMENT. SORRY TO LEAVE A MESS—
—BUT I DON'T HAVE TIME RIGHT NOW.

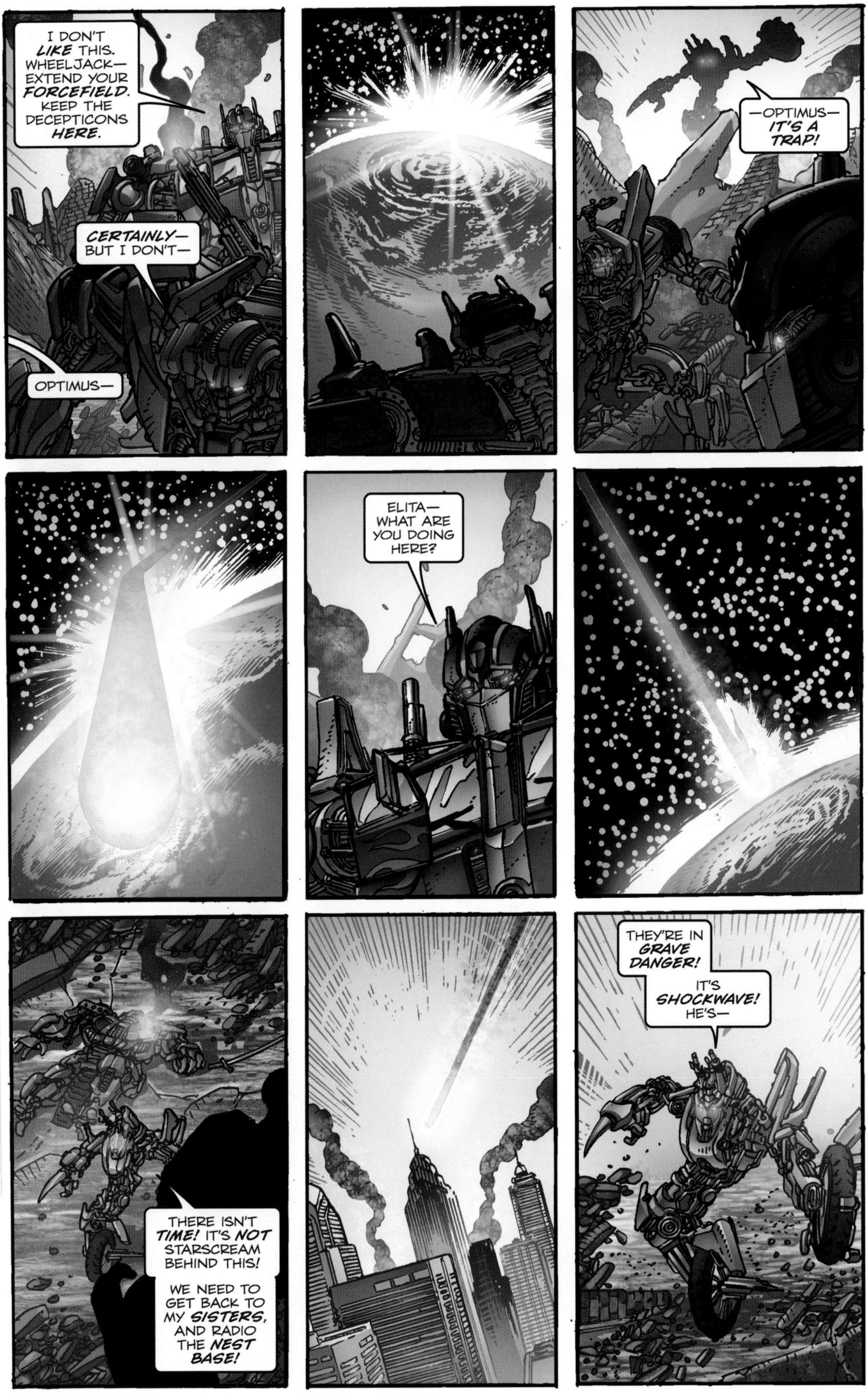
I DON'T LIKE THIS. WHEELJACK— EXTEND YOUR FORCEFIELD. KEEP THE DECEPTICONS HERE.
CERTAINLY— BUT I DON'T—
OPTIMUS—
—OPTIMUS— IT'S A TRAP!
ELITA— WHAT ARE YOU DOING HERE?
THERE ISN'T TIME! IT'S NOT STARSCREAM BEHIND THIS!
WE NEED TO GET BACK TO MY SISTERS, AND RADIO THE NEST BASE!
THEY'RE IN GRAVE DANGER!
IT'S SHOCKWAVE! HE'S—

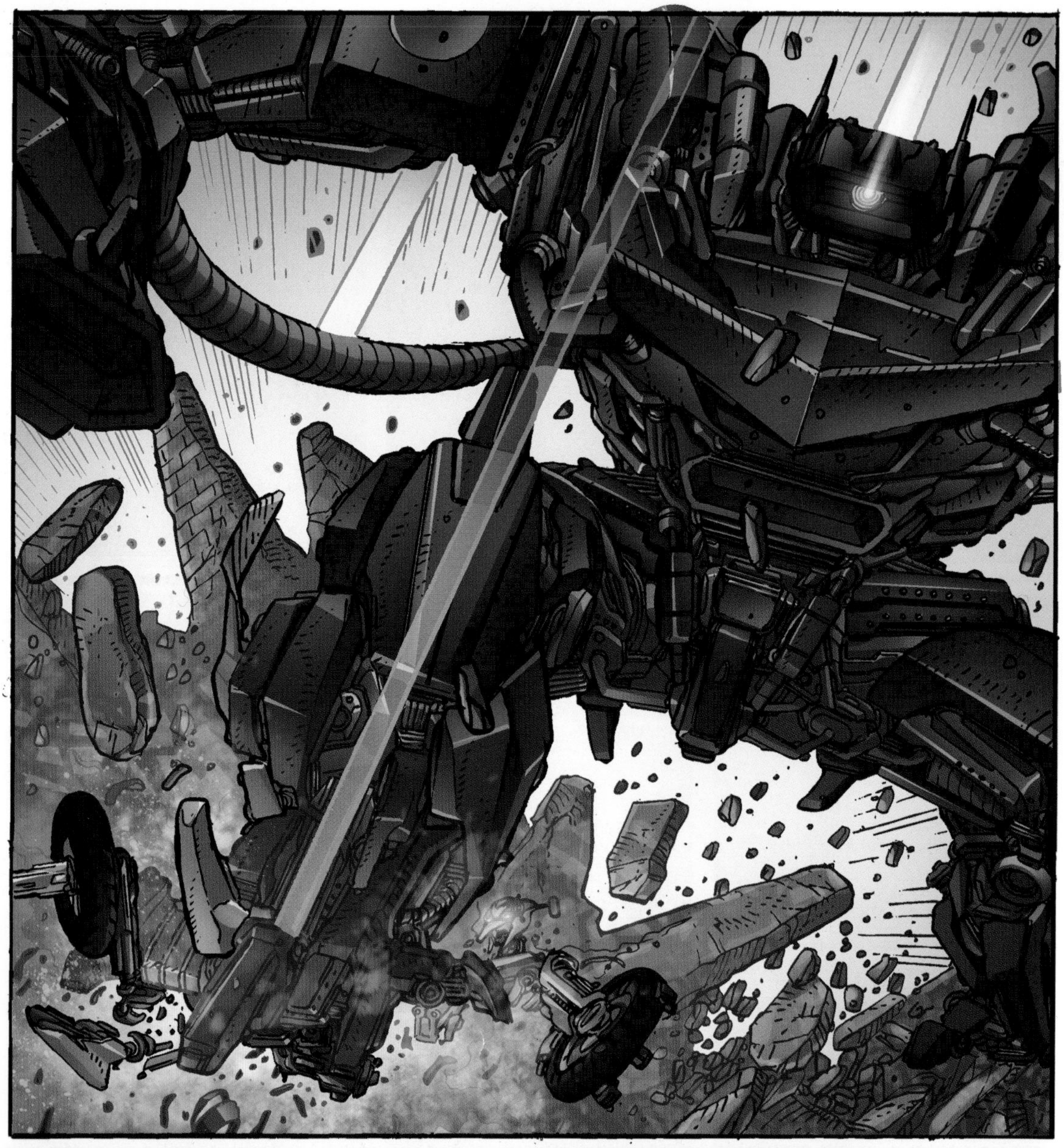

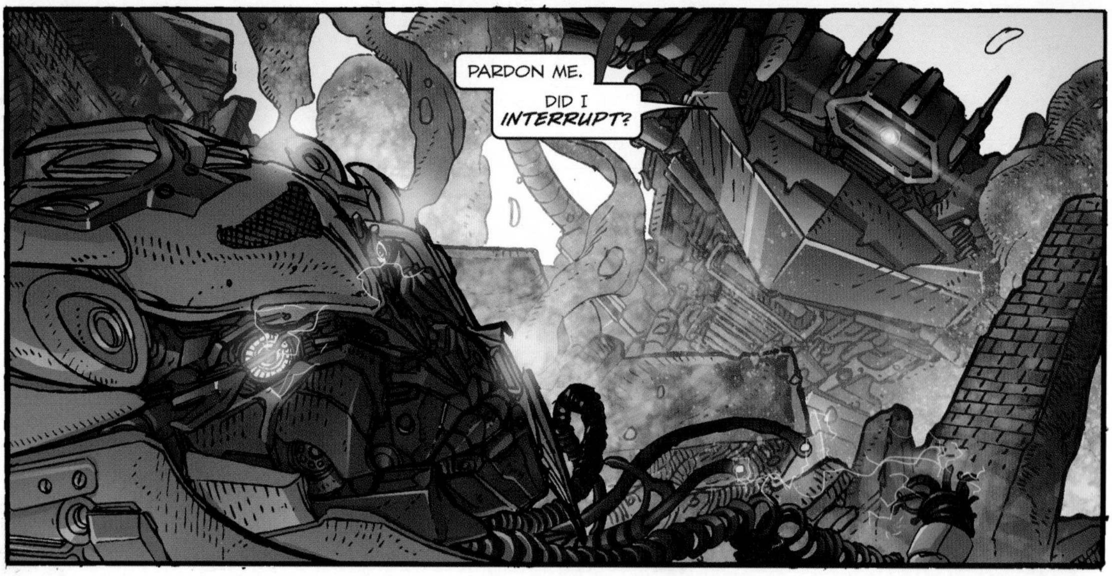
PARDON ME.
DID I INTERRUPT?

AIIIGGGHH!

EEIIIAAHHHH!

ELITA...

...I COULD FEEL HER...

...DYING...

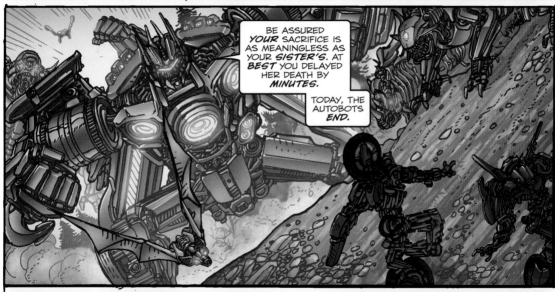

BE ASSURED *YOUR* SACRIFICE IS AS MEANINGLESS AS YOUR *SISTER'S.* AT *BEST* YOU DELAYED HER DEATH BY *MINUTES.*

TODAY, THE AUTOBOTS *END.*

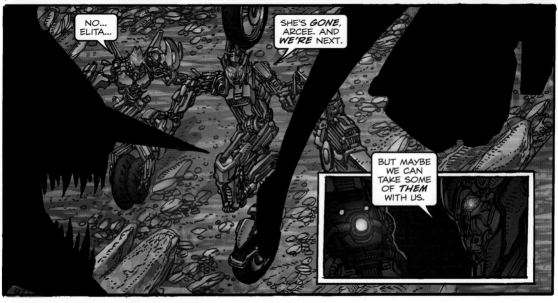

NO... ELITA...

SHE'S *GONE,* ARCEE. AND *WE'RE* NEXT.

BUT MAYBE WE CAN TAKE SOME OF *THEM* WITH US.

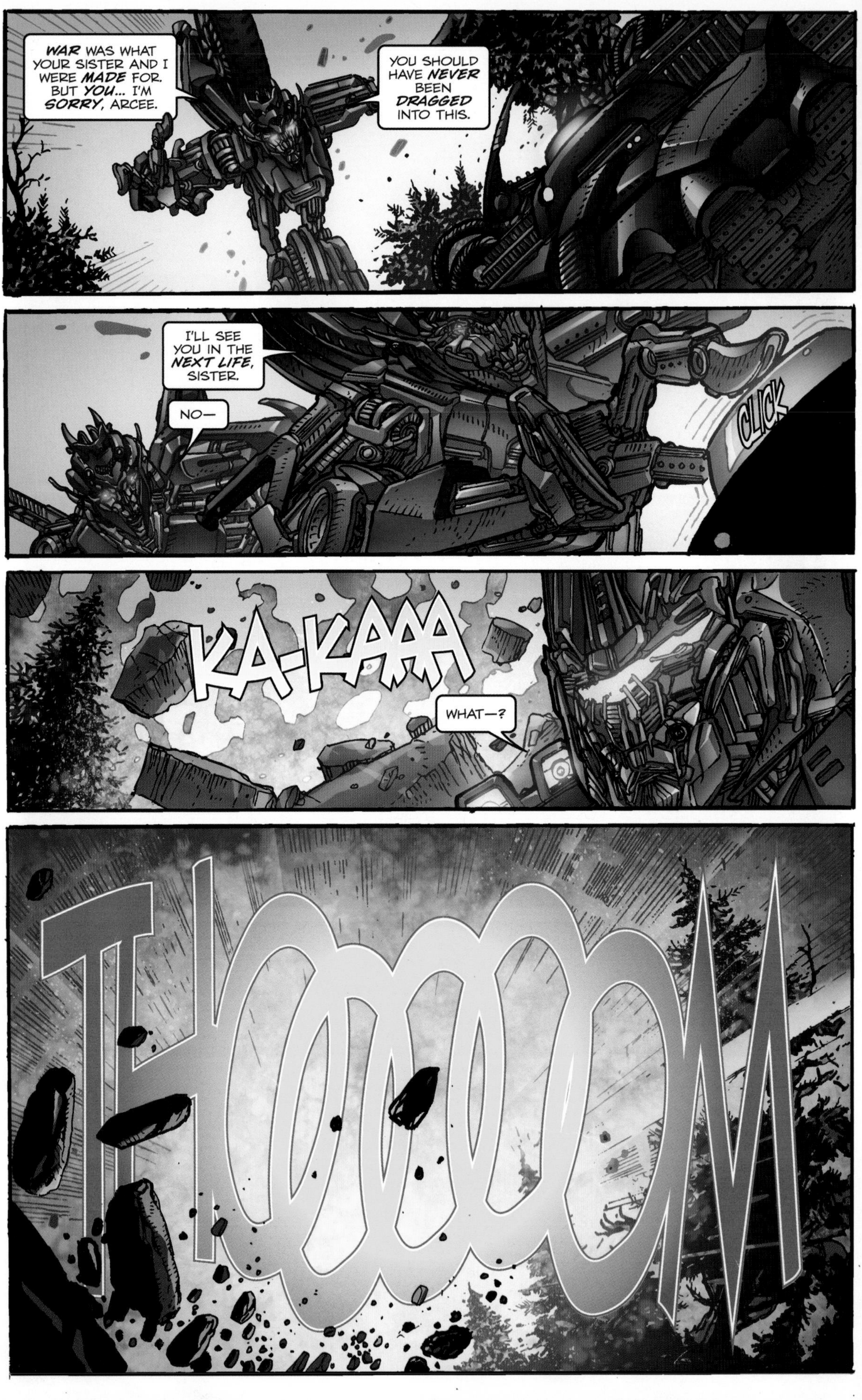
WAR WAS WHAT YOUR SISTER AND I WERE MADE FOR. BUT YOU... I'M SORRY, ARCEE.
YOU SHOULD HAVE NEVER BEEN DRAGGED INTO THIS.
I'LL SEE YOU IN THE NEXT LIFE, SISTER.
NO—
CLICK
KA-KAAA
WHAT—?
THOOOOOM

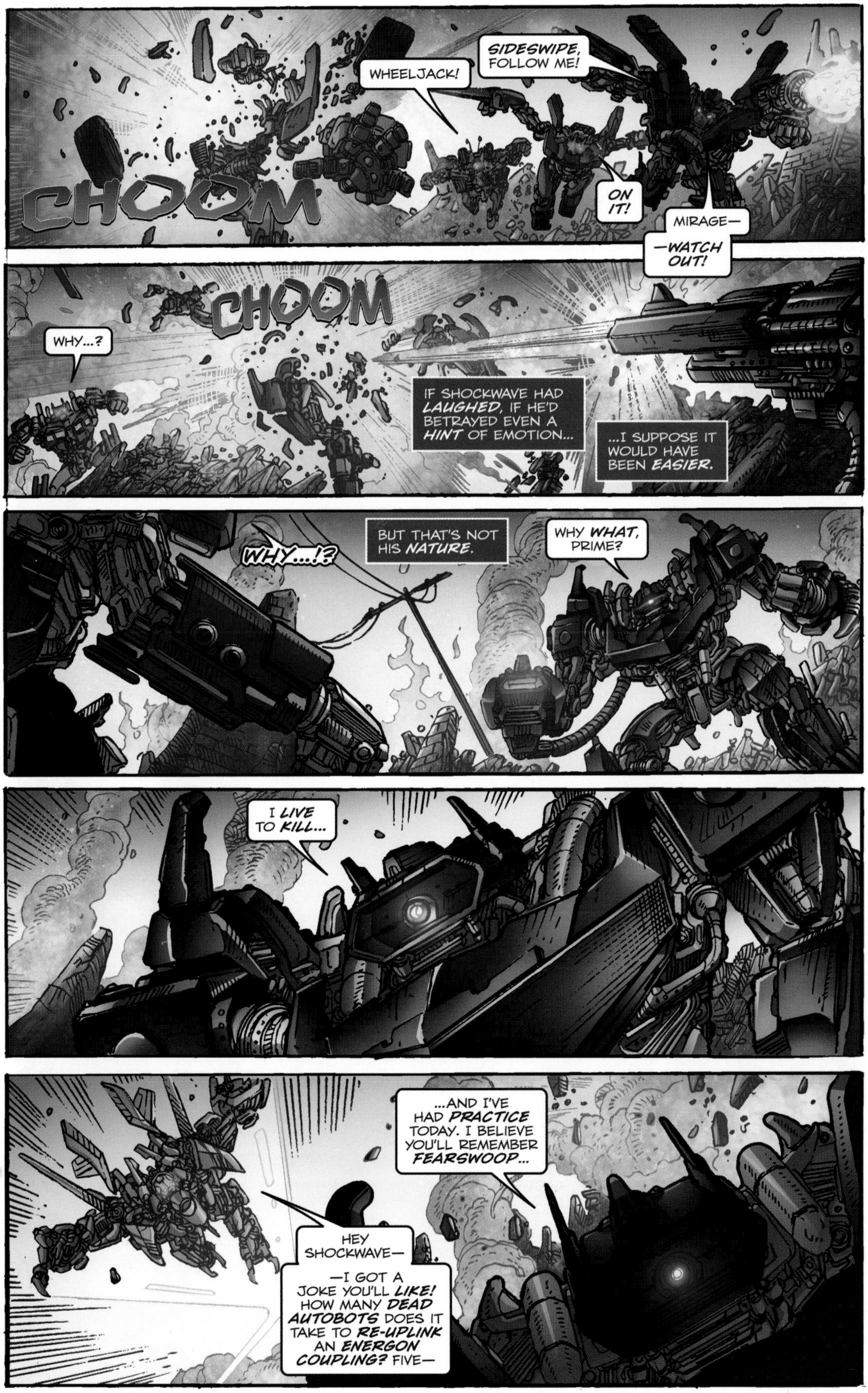
CHOOM
WHEELJACK!
SIDESWIPE, FOLLOW ME!
ON IT!
MIRAGE—
—WATCH OUT!
CHOOM
WHY...?
IF SHOCKWAVE HAD LAUGHED, IF HE'D BETRAYED EVEN A HINT OF EMOTION...
...I SUPPOSE IT WOULD HAVE BEEN EASIER.
WHY...!?
BUT THAT'S NOT HIS NATURE.
WHY WHAT, PRIME?
I LIVE TO KILL...
...AND I'VE HAD PRACTICE TODAY. I BELIEVE YOU'LL REMEMBER FEARSWOOP...
HEY SHOCKWAVE—
—I GOT A JOKE YOU'LL LIKE! HOW MANY DEAD AUTOBOTS DOES IT TAKE TO RE-UPLINK AN ENERGON COUPLING? FIVE—

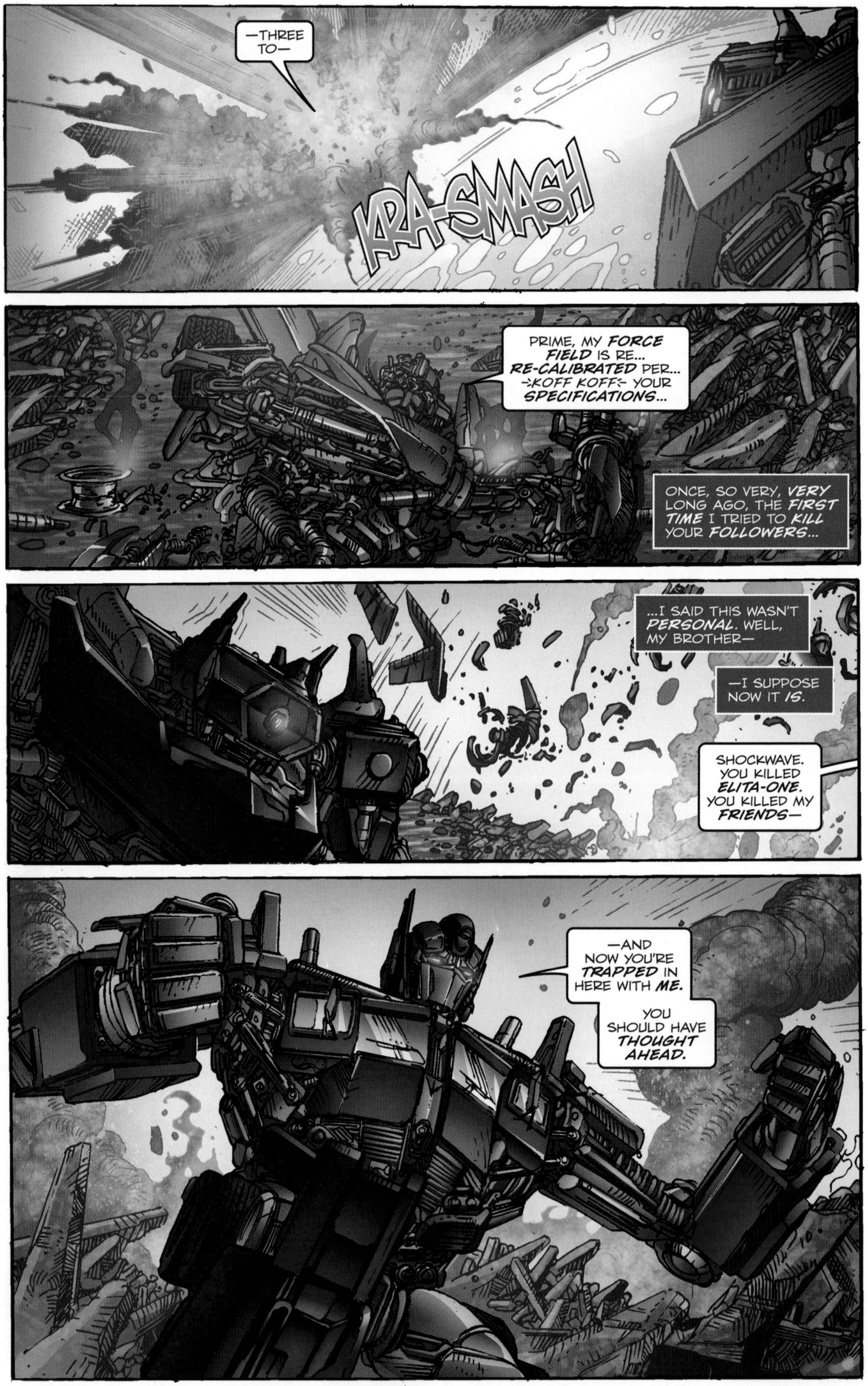
—THREE TO—
KRA-SMASH
PRIME, MY FORCE FIELD IS RE... RE-CALIBRATED PER... -KOFF KOFF- YOUR SPECIFICATIONS...
ONCE, SO VERY, VERY LONG AGO, THE FIRST TIME I TRIED TO KILL YOUR FOLLOWERS...
...I SAID THIS WASN'T PERSONAL. WELL, MY BROTHER—
—I SUPPOSE NOW IT IS.
SHOCKWAVE. YOU KILLED ELITA-ONE. YOU KILLED MY FRIENDS—
—AND NOW YOU'RE TRAPPED IN HERE WITH ME.
YOU SHOULD HAVE THOUGHT AHEAD.

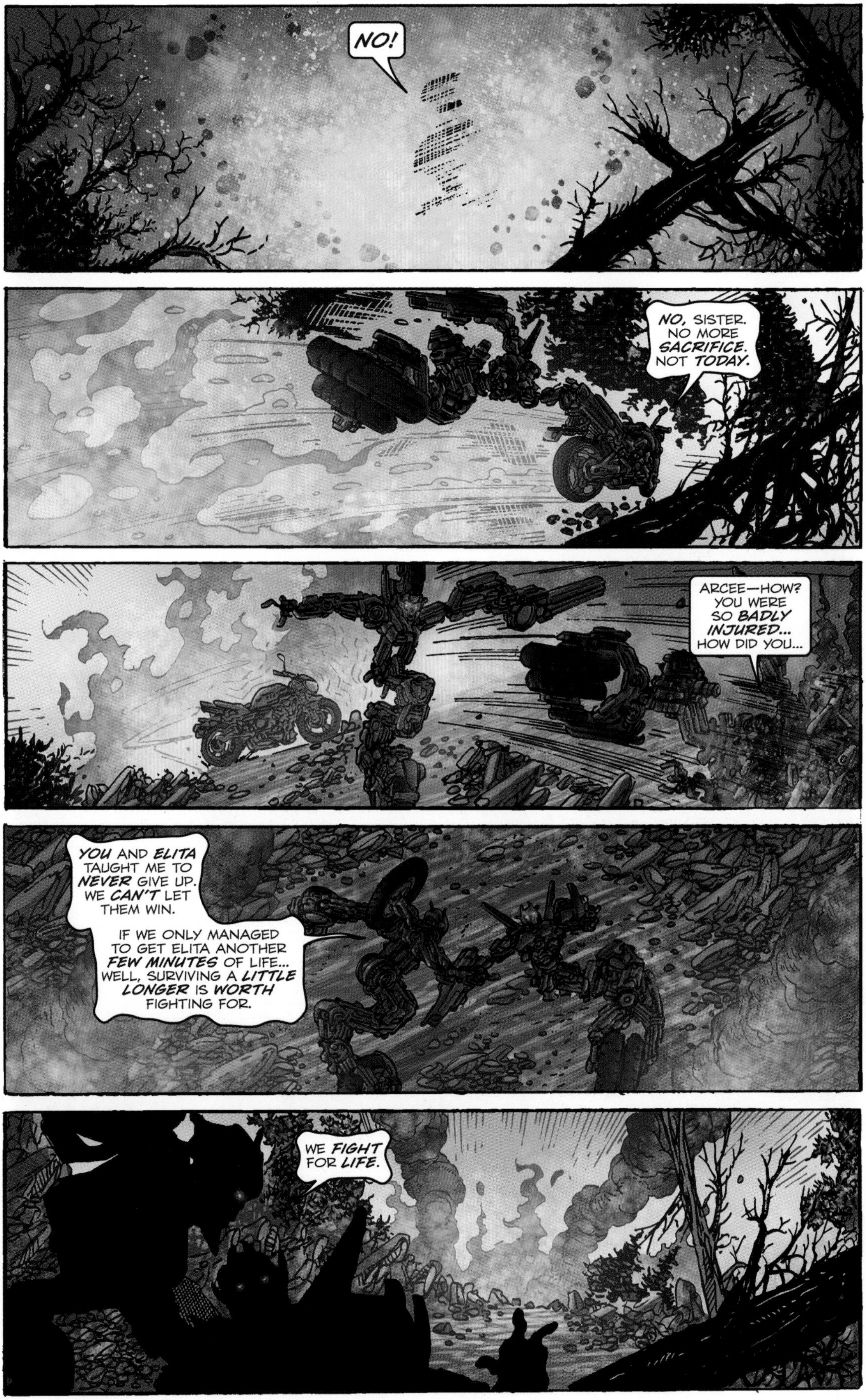
NO!
NO, SISTER. NO MORE SACRIFICE. NOT TODAY.
ARCEE—HOW? YOU WERE SO BADLY INJURED... HOW DID YOU...
YOU AND ELITA TAUGHT ME TO NEVER GIVE UP. WE CAN'T LET THEM WIN.
IF WE ONLY MANAGED TO GET ELITA ANOTHER FEW MINUTES OF LIFE... WELL, SURVIVING A LITTLE LONGER IS WORTH FIGHTING FOR.
WE FIGHT FOR LIFE.

AUTOBOTS— *NO ONE WALKS AWAY FROM THIS!*
WHAT? BUT—
—THIS WAS MY *MOMENT* OF *TRIUMPH!*
WHAM
—*NEVER!*
YOUR KIND WILL *NEVER* WIN, SHOCKWAVE—
KKRASCH

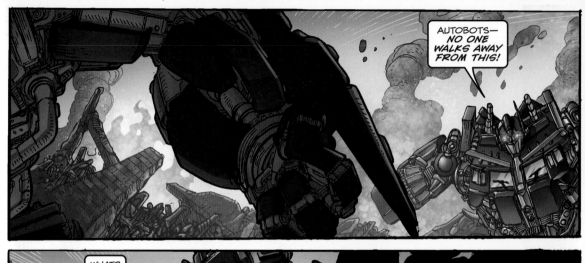

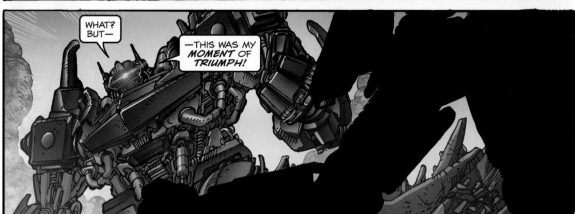

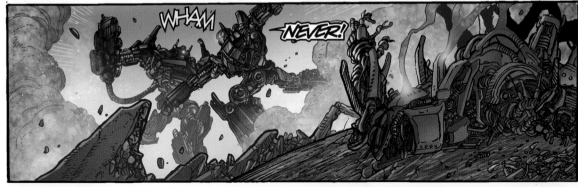

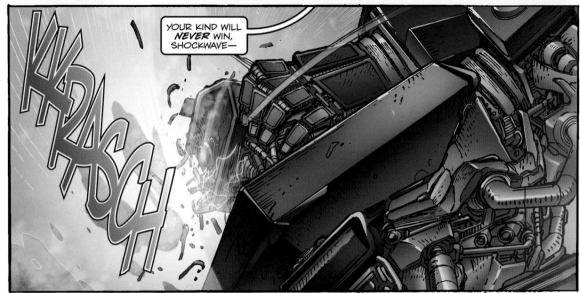

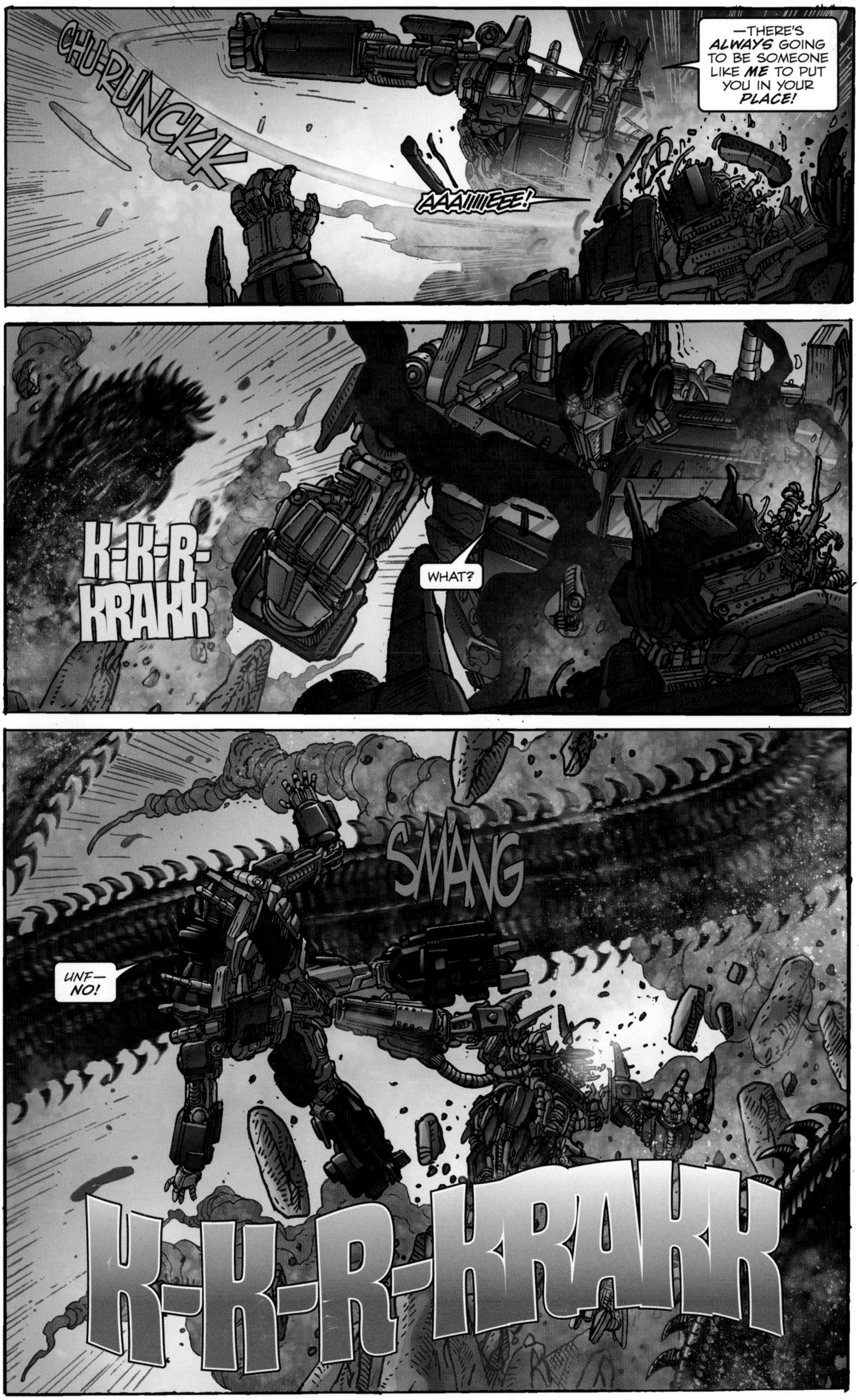
CHU-RUNCKK
—THERE'S *ALWAYS* GOING TO BE SOMEONE LIKE *ME* TO PUT YOU IN YOUR *PLACE!*
AAAIIIIEEE!
K-K-R-KRAKK
WHAT?
SMANG
UNF— NO!
K-K-R-KRAKK

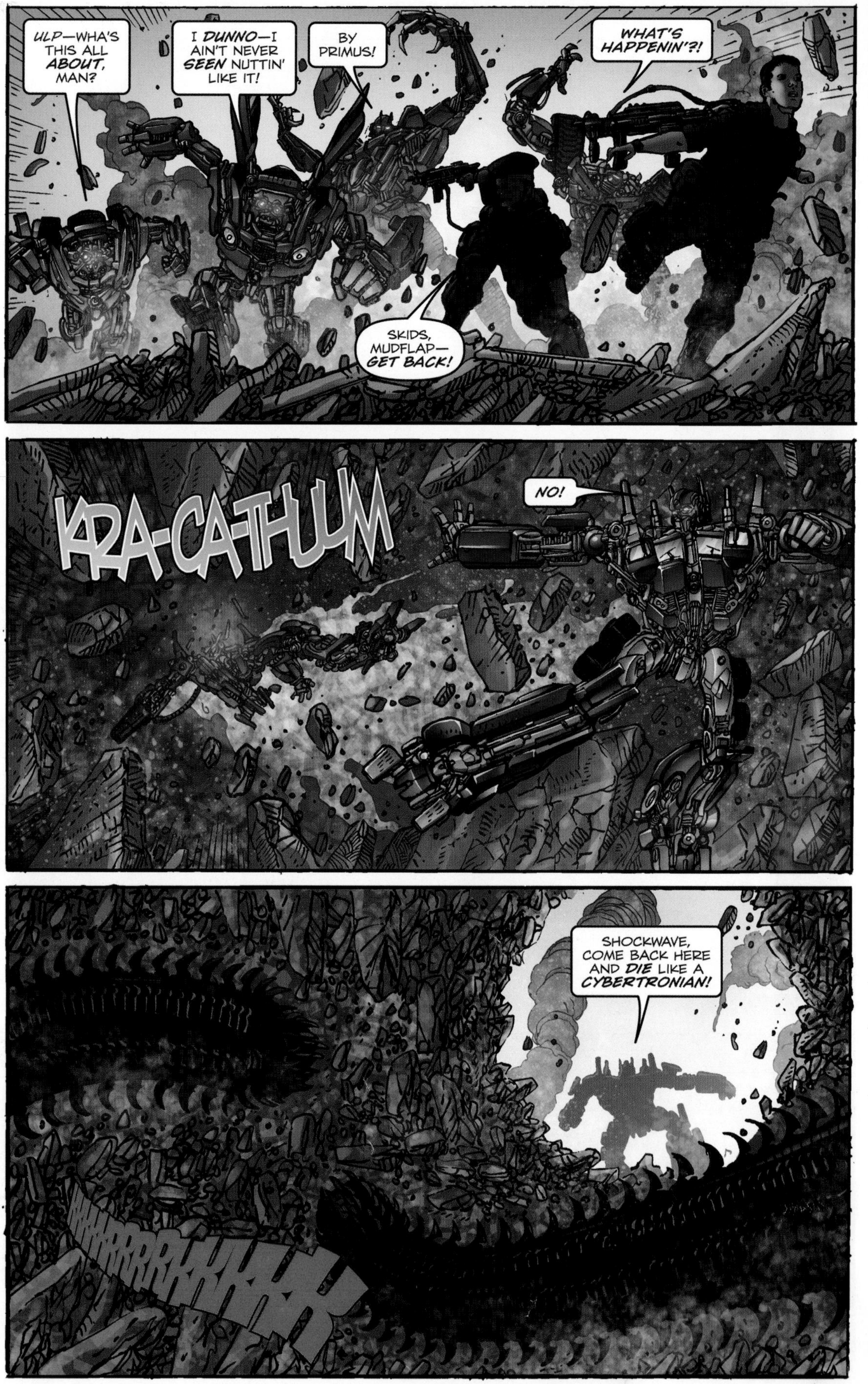
ULP—WHA'S THIS ALL ABOUT, MAN?
I DUNNO—I AIN'T NEVER SEEN NUTTIN' LIKE IT!
BY PRIMUS!
WHAT'S HAPPENIN'?!
SKIDS, MUDFLAP—GET BACK!
KRA-CA-THUUM
NO!
SHOCKWAVE, COME BACK HERE AND DIE LIKE A CYBERTRONIAN!

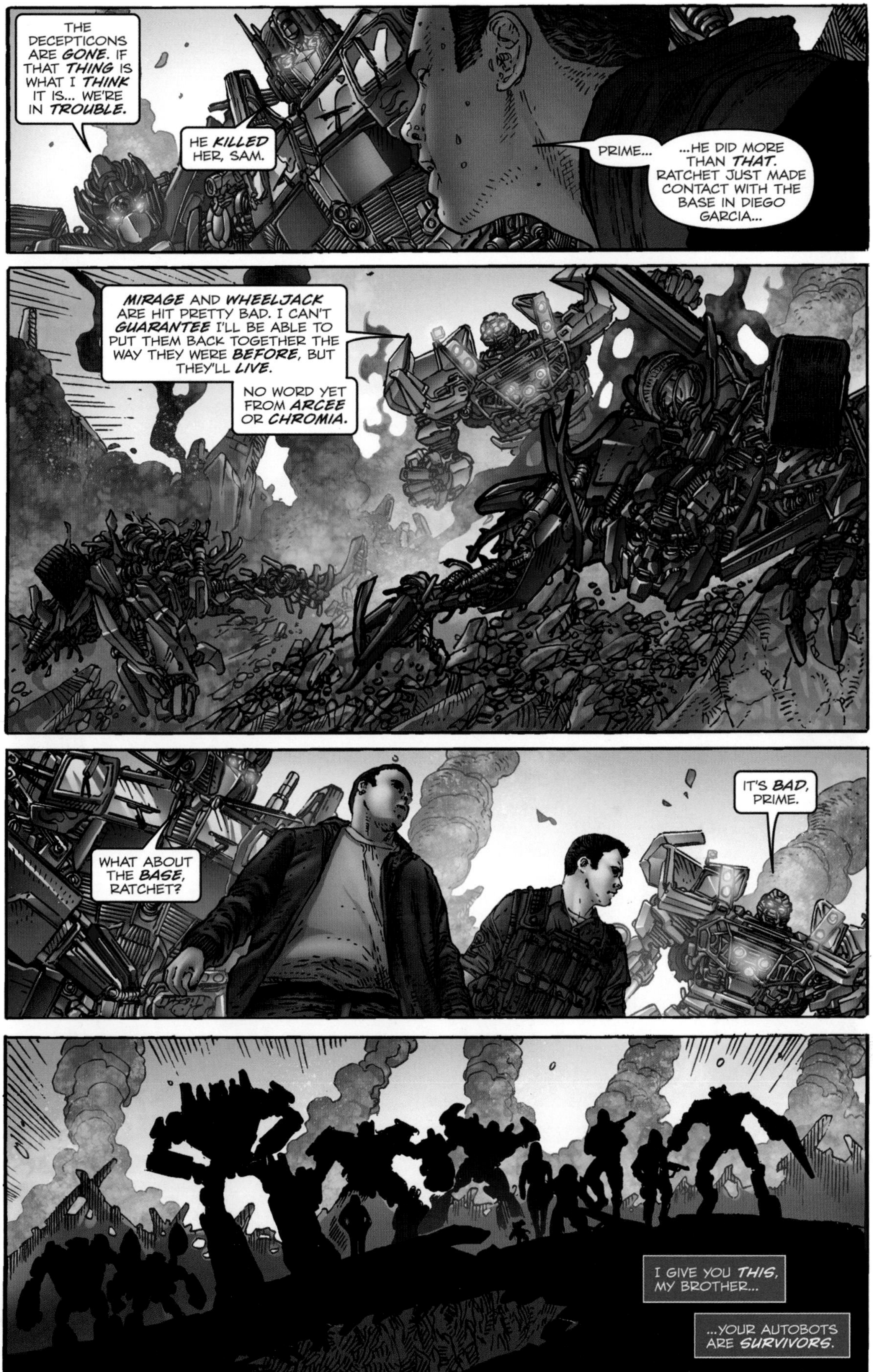
THE DECEPTICONS ARE GONE. IF THAT THING IS WHAT I THINK IT IS... WE'RE IN TROUBLE.
HE KILLED HER, SAM.
PRIME...
...HE DID MORE THAN THAT. RATCHET JUST MADE CONTACT WITH THE BASE IN DIEGO GARCIA...
MIRAGE AND WHEELJACK ARE HIT PRETTY BAD. I CAN'T GUARANTEE I'LL BE ABLE TO PUT THEM BACK TOGETHER THE WAY THEY WERE BEFORE, BUT THEY'LL LIVE.
NO WORD YET FROM ARCEE OR CHROMIA.
WHAT ABOUT THE BASE, RATCHET?
IT'S BAD, PRIME.
I GIVE YOU THIS, MY BROTHER...
...YOUR AUTOBOTS ARE SURVIVORS.

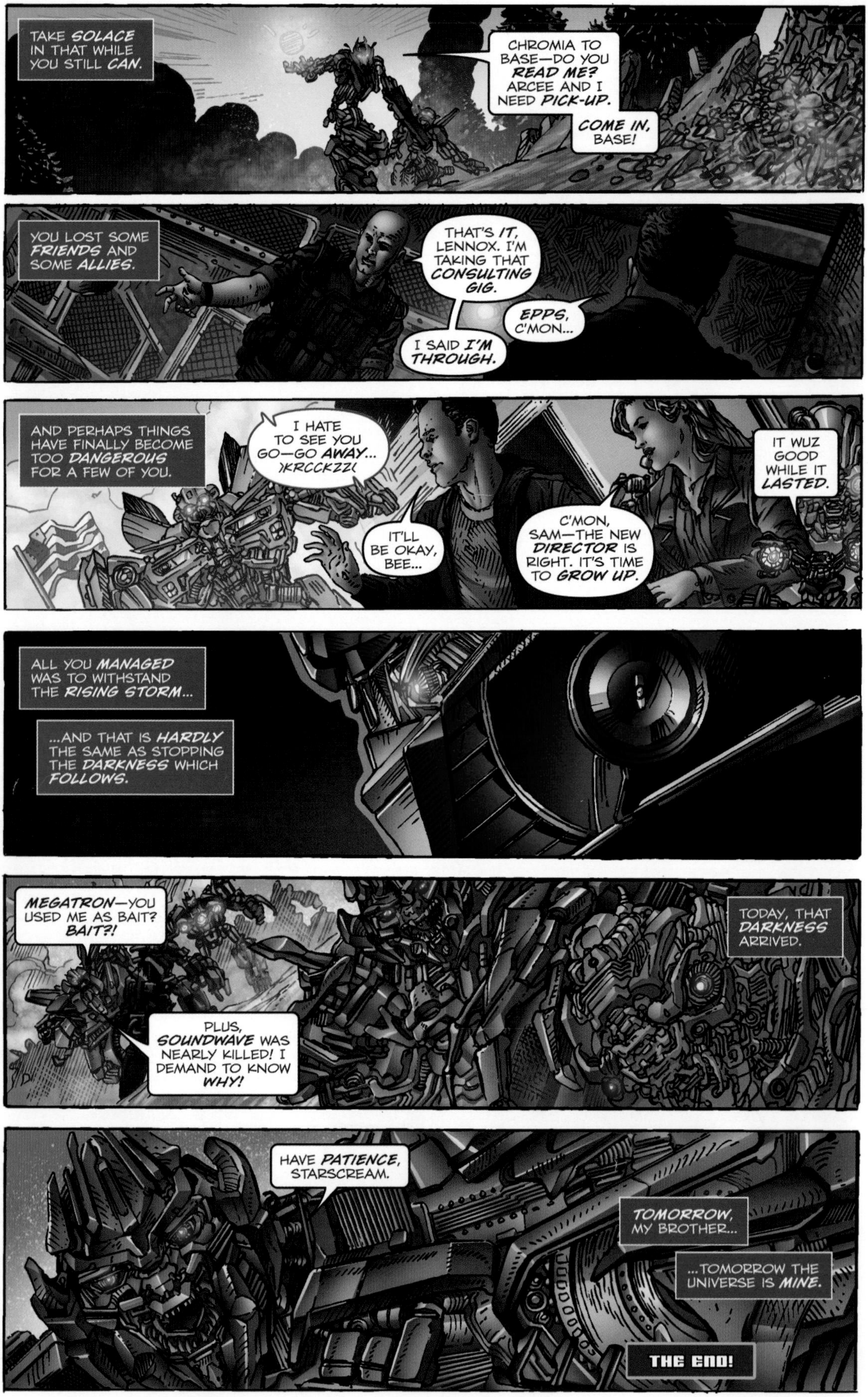
TAKE SOLACE IN THAT WHILE YOU STILL CAN.
CHROMIA TO BASE—DO YOU READ ME? ARCEE AND I NEED PICK-UP.
COME IN, BASE!
YOU LOST SOME FRIENDS AND SOME ALLIES.
THAT'S IT, LENNOX. I'M TAKING THAT CONSULTING GIG.
EPPS, C'MON...
I SAID I'M THROUGH.
AND PERHAPS THINGS HAVE FINALLY BECOME TOO DANGEROUS FOR A FEW OF YOU.
I HATE TO SEE YOU GO—GO AWAY...)KRCCKZZ(
IT'LL BE OKAY, BEE...
C'MON, SAM—THE NEW DIRECTOR IS RIGHT. IT'S TIME TO GROW UP.
IT WUZ GOOD WHILE IT LASTED.
ALL YOU MANAGED WAS TO WITHSTAND THE RISING STORM...
...AND THAT IS HARDLY THE SAME AS STOPPING THE DARKNESS WHICH FOLLOWS.
MEGATRON—YOU USED ME AS BAIT? BAIT?!
PLUS, SOUNDWAVE WAS NEARLY KILLED! I DEMAND TO KNOW WHY!
TODAY, THAT DARKNESS ARRIVED.
HAVE PATIENCE, STARSCREAM.
TOMORROW, MY BROTHER...
...TOMORROW THE UNIVERSE IS MINE.
THE END!